California Wear

BY SIL STUBB

DORRANCE
PUBLISHING CO
EST. 1920
PITTSBURGH, PENNSYLVANIA 15238

Dorrance Publishing Co
585 Alpha Drive
Suite 103
Pittsburgh, PA 15238
Visit our website at www.dorrancebookstore.com

ISBN: 979-8-8892-5418-8
eISBN: 979-8-8892-5918-3

California Wear

Dedication

For my family

Acknowledgements

Thanks to the world wide web

Table of Contents

Chapter 1: Gabby

Gabby is named after a writer. Author Gabriella Day was a romance novelist. Her mother read many books by that author while she was pregnant with Gabby. Gabby's mother loved the novelist's name. She named her daughter after her idol.

Gabby meets a boy at a coffee shop. She gives him her phone number.

He calls her and asks her out on a date.

They date each other for 8 months until he dials her number one day to tell her that he's not interested in something serious yet and would like to break up with her.

Gabby takes the news well and figures she'll find love sometime later in life.

When Gabby told her mother that she had broken up with her boyfriend, her mother looked at her sadly and said, "I thought you two were going to get married for sure. You must be devastated!"

Gabby replied, "Well, he's not the only fish in the sea. I'll find someone else."

Chapter 2: The Career

Gabby loves her job. She started working at the fashion retailer two years ago.

During her interview she just acted like her normal self. She was cute.

She loved to talk and made conversation easily. She was a brunette with short and straight hair.

During her interview she wore overalls like she was farming for a job. She hadn't really considered working at that place until she opened the building's tall glass doors.

The glassy front stood to cover a spacious cream laminate flooring that extended inside a deep mecca of clothes. The walls were covered with fashion from ceiling to floor.

She entered to speak to the manager about getting a position at the flashy establishment.

She didn't prepare too much for the interview, but she had some previous experience at landing a job. When the manager told her she was hired, she smiled from her left to her right cheek. She felt thrilled. Dressing in style was one of her favorite hobbies.

Her job was to open the front entry door for all the customers that came in.

She had to greet them. "Hi! Welcome to California Wear!" Gabby would announce this to all the customers that walked in.

She worked at the department store retailer for six months greeting customers. Her attitude was on point. As the customers approached, she never forgot to give her smile in the greeting.

After six months, her store manager asked her to come into his office so they could discuss how she was doing in the company.

Her store manager gave her a promotion. Gabby was promoted into cash handling.

Chapter 3: Promotion

Gabby could see from the cash register another employee that worked with her. He was the only guy on the sales floor that wasn't a manager. She caught him peeking at her from a distance. She thought he was kind of cute. It was mostly girls there at that chic clothing retailer. The place she was working at was called, California Wear. He dressed nice. His shirt looked like it was freshly pressed, and he wore a tie.

She thought he had flushed a little while he met her gaze.

Or maybe he had just drank down some hot coffee.

She wasn't sure. Gabby decided to keep to herself. She was engaging enough with the customers that came to buy stuff.

Another six months passed, and she had been introduced to Tommy.

Tommy was the guy who always came in wearing freshly pressed shirts.

Tommy had a great sense of humor. He approached Gabby one day to relay a message to Gabby. He said that the store manager wanted to see her in his office.

Tommy told her while she was standing in front of the cash register, "The manager wants you to come to his office for a minute. He said he would like to talk to you."

Gabby went to the manager's office.

Once she came in, she sat down on the swivel chair.

The conversation was pleasant. Her manager was happy with her.

"I've been hearing only good things about you." He complimented her.

He told her the management staff were considering a person to promote. He told Gabby that he was sure she was the right person for the job.

He said, "Welcome to sales at California Wear, Gabby. Are you happy?"

Gabby answered, "Yes! I'm very happy about this! Thank you, sir!"

Chapter 4: Work

Selling clothes was really the dream. Gabby loved all the fashion. She could guess the size people were by just looking at them. She kept her department organized. She loved dressing the mannequin.

Her manager thought she was doing a great job. When Gabby's manager called her customers for feedback on Gabby's performance, the manager only got five-star reviews in response.

Gabby's work schedule increased. She had gone from an 8-hour work day to a 12-hour work day.

She would sit at work thinking about how she hadn't found someone to love yet.

Work was life. There was little time to chat with anyone outside of work.

She would pull up to the California Wear clothing retail building in her two-door Mini Cooper, lock up her car, and within seconds sign in to work.

She took her ten-minute breaks outside the rear door of the building. Gabby would light up a long cigarette and smoke it to the ring. Her co-worker Tommy would occasionally join her.

Chapter 5: Winter

It was close to Christmas. The weather was chill. The warm California Wear clothing line was out hanging on the sales floor.

The Monday morning meeting announced a yearly occurrence.

The manager shouted, "Alright everyone, this Friday we will begin inventory. Some of us are required to stay past their regular shift and work a second shift overnight. There will be a second wave once the overnight shift goes home. I'll be handing out inventory schedules once the meeting is over."

Chapter 6: Overnighter

For Gabby, this was her second time doing inventory. Gabby thought that inventory was hard work, but working in the middle of night was sort of fun. She felt like she was having a big slumber party while in her California Wear clothing line's version of an asymmetric ruffled tux blazer in black. She worked drunk with sleepiness sipping on large coffees to beat the haziness.

The first overnight inventory's 10-minute break arrived.

Gabby went outside to the front parking lot that was deserted for the most part. There were five cars parked in the best spots. Their trunks and driver's side doors were open. Derrick— the new hire— had his stereo on, blasting energetic dance music. It was 2 in the morning, but the mood was very cheery. Gabby smoked her cigarette in a place she normally didn't get to.

Inventory ended at 9 A.M. Gabby drove herself home and went to sleep.

Chapter 7: Management

It's the beginning of the year, and Gabby's department is in need of a new floor manager. Gabby is almost sure the job is going to be offered to her. Her floor manager had only been giving her high fives and high remarks on all her performance reviews. Her regular floor manager had just transferred to another store, and management needed a new replacement.

During the first week of the month of May, her presence is requested in the store management's office. When she went inside the office, she received the news that she would be the new manager of her department.

Gabby's was officially promoted, and she would be earning a salary. She is extremely pleased. There was nothing Gabby wanted more.

Chapter 8: All Work

Gabby seldom spent time at home. Her relationship with her mother had been deteriorating. Her mother's patience had become very thin.

She got up in the morning, ate a light breakfast, and left for work. She didn't do any chores anymore. She only came home to sleep.

Her progression at her job was mostly a secret she unintentionally kept from her mom. Gabby never sat down to talk to her parents about what was happening in her life.

Her dating life was non-existent. She never brought a boy home.

Her family could see that there was no sight of a marriage in the near future.

Chapter 9: The Fight

As time passed and Gabby worked her long shifts as the manager in her department, she would arrive at home unannounced and go straight to the kitchen's stove. She would pick some food directly off the cooking pot to eat, then go to her room to sleep without having said a word to anyone else in the house.

Her mother was beginning to feel increasingly aggravated.

It was the Saturday evening that marked Gabby's second year working at the clothing retailer when a memorable fight between Gabby and her mother took place. Gabby had just arrived at home back from work. Once Gabby walked in, she was headed straight for the kitchen. While Gabby was in the kitchen was when her mother rushed towards her and said, "What do you think this is? A hotel? You come in and sleep! That's it!"

Her mother screamed and taunted Gabby for several minutes, "You don't get to do this! Just come home, walk in, eat, then go to sleep! You don't even cook! You expect me to do everything around here?"

Gabby had walked into the kitchen, like usual, to grab food. Her mother followed her and continued. "Don't you think you should do something around here?"

Chapter 10: The Move

Gabby's relationship with her mother was in chaos. Gabby was feeling like she needed to stop being a bother.

She decided to move out. She got into a heavy discussion with her mom and she told her that she was going to be leaving the house to move out to another place.

When her next day off cycled around, she grabbed a few of her essential things from her room to finally check out of that so-called hotel.

She decided to find a nicer hotel.

Chapter 11: The Hotel

She checks into a much nicer hotel. It's in the downtown of a very famous city. In a very busy section of town. It's a hotel she's heard of over the radio and from other people's gossip.

The hotel has a doorman dressed in what resembles royal British attire. The outside stands high with 21 floors of a cemented façade.

Walking inside the tall building presents ornate coffered ceilings. She decided to stay long term.

She was going to continue to work at her job during the day, and in the evening she was going to commute back to her new home, her own room at the hotel building.

Chapter 12: Basketball Player

On her first night at the hotel's sitting area, she meets a basketball player named Toby.

It's a Friday night, and Toby tells Gabby that he's there for the basketball conference that will be taking place over the weekend.

Toby likes Gabby from the start. She's beautiful, she's sweet, and she's available. They hook up that night.

Chapter 13: Days Off

The guests at that hotel stay there for the night, some for a few nights, and others for a few months.

Some of the guests work all day and just come to their rooms to sleep at night.

There were various rooms to choose from. Small, medium, or large. The prices varied upon size.

The day that Gabby had checked in, she was really distraught. She was upset about the fight she just had with her mother and told the hotel front desk that she just wanted a small room she could stay in for an extended amount of time.

Gabby stayed in one of the better priced rooms. The lowest of the pricing scale. It was small yet nice looking. The bed was soft and extremely comfortable. There was a one-seat sofa loveseat in the room.

She worked all day and came to her room at night.

Breakfast was at the eatery conjoined to the hotel. It was on the hotel's first floor. On her days off she would lounge around the hotel halls or sit at the bar having a soda.

Chapter 14: Halls

On a Wednesday night Gabby takes a drink from the bar and decides to explore the other floors of the hotel.

She calls the elevator and waits. Once the elevator arrives, she gets inside it with her drink. She looks towards the floor buttons and swirls her index finger over the numbers.

She considers to herself, "Which floor shall I pick...?" She notices that there is no 13th floor.

She presses the 14th floor key. The elevator makes the trip up slowly. She sips her drink. The elevator passes the 12th floor and stops directly at the 14th floor without an in-between. Once the doors open on the 14th floor she gets out.

She walks down the hall sipping on her martini.

Walking down the hall she sees a hotel cleaning lady busy inside a room.

The sheets of a large queen size bed are being changed. The bed's headboard is musical in design. It's filled with vine like waves as if they are ledger lines of a music sheet but growing some leaves. The bed's head board stands tall against the room's back wall. She passes by the room after a few moments.

There is a man further down the hall getting ready to enter his room. He is tall and has an olive complexion.

He is sliding his key over the key pad until he notices her standing and looking directly at him.

He slightly waves to her and motions to start a conversation. He says, "Hi! I'm Johnathan. What's your name?"

The male guest looks friendly and nice enough to talk to.

Gabby leans on the wall of the hallway and says, "I'm Gabby. I'm staying here at the hotel."

Johnathan says, "Would you like to come in for a moment?" He points towards the inside of his room.

Gabby says, "Sure. I guess just for a moment."

Johnathan's look was intense. He was a lean man. He flashed sincerity with his eyes. He was easy going with his movements. After he let her into his room, he proceeded to close the door behind him and approach her suggestively.

Once he comes inside the room he sits down. He says, "I've seen you here at the hotel before. You're kind of cute."

He was back from his long day at work. He really liked getting some feminine attention. He asked, "Do you want to make out?"

She replied, "Sure."

He got up to approach her. He kissed her lips. They got it on right away. They kissed for some time until that led to the bed.

Chapter 15: Room 613

A woman walks up a short but wide set of stairs to approach the hotel's second-floor bar. The long bar stands on the back wall of the second floor facing the top of the stairs. She takes a seat from a row of seats colored in a deep wood color. These seats were more like high chairs covered in white leather cushions.

The bar slab is smooth onyx marble. It shined like it had recently been wiped clean.

The woman that had approached the bar is tense but extremely well-dressed. Gabby had been sitting two chairs away on another high chair since before the woman had sat down next to her.

The mysterious woman had the smell of perfume on her. Its scent had the strongest sweet smell and suffocated Gabby in the mildest of ways.

The mysterious woman orders a drink from the bartender, "White Russian on the rocks, please?"

The bartender turns to his bottles. The large selection of alcoholic potions was separated into sections.

The back wall has mirrors reflecting back a cascade of booze. The bartender walks to where his liqueurs are sectioned and selects a fitting booze maker. He mixes it with some cream over ice and adds some minor touches in preparation to hand the lady a drink.

Once the drink arrives, she takes a sip. She says to the bartender, "Put it on room 613's tab, please." Then she places a five on the counter. She picks up the napkin and the glass.

Gabby heard the woman tell the bartender that she had been staying in room 613.

The woman approaches Gabby's chair while holding her drink. The woman in room 613 asks Gabby, "Do you know Johnathan?"

Gabby reflected on her steamy first night she had with Johnathan behind the closed door of his high-priced room with a view of the lit-up city. That had been two months ago. Johnathan, like her and apparently this other woman as well, were extended stay guests of the hotel.

Johnathan had revealed to Gabby that he was a salesman too. Just like Gabby. She felt she was deep in love with him now.

She replied, "Yes. Why? Do you know him?"

The woman answers, "I've been desiring him for a long time. I've been wanting to go out with him since long before you met him, I believe. You met him just recently, right? I've been here longer. One year now. I suggest you break up with him."

Chapter 16: Refusal

It seemed like the woman staying in room 613 was an extended stay guest that had been at the hotel longer than Gabby. She, Johnathan, and the woman in room 613 were marinating at the hotel for several months. Gabby suddenly recalls seeing her around the halls from time to time. Gabby is caught off guard by the woman's revelation and is appalled by her demand.

Gabby affirms her, "No. I'm not breaking up with him!"

The woman from room 613 is standing next Gabby still holding her drink and her napkin. She decides to retreat and walks back to her seat two chairs away.

Gabby turns away while still seated in her seat. She continues to sip her cocktail.

The mysterious woman from room 613 appears not to mind Gabby's presence any longer.

Gabby decides to turn in and heads up to her room on the third floor.

Chapter 17: Mystery Man

One evening Gabby was spending time with Johnathan. She's sipping on a cocktail from the hotel bar while in his room, and she decides to pry into his character a little further. She decided to ask him what he wanted in life. She was sitting on his bed facing him when she said, "What do think your destiny in life is? I mean, do you want to be a father? How about what do you think about being in a committed relationship?"

The dark-haired, olive-skinned male replied, "I'm not interested in a real relationship right now, I think I'm waiting for the right girl still."

Gabby was shocked. She didn't like his response. She felt the rejection. He admitted that he didn't want to marry yet. He didn't say it, but he implied it. He told her that she wasn't the right girl.

She felt she should wait too. She would wait until she met the right person too.

She would wait until she met someone that felt that she was quality material too. The kind that is worthy of commitment.

It clearly seemed that her relationship with him was over.

Gabby said to him, "I get it, not me, right? I guess it's better to call it quits now then." She hastily makes her way out of his room feeling a little ashamed. She thinks to herself, "What does he think I am? Trash? A tramp? A waste of a person?" She feels gloomy. She feels resentment.

As she reaches the elevators, she sees a man standing further down the hall.

He is wearing a hotel worker outfit. A dress shirt, a black vest, black slacks, and black dress shoes. It looks like a uniform.

It looks like the common wear of the workers around the hotel building. He's young. Her appears to be around her age. He's godly handsome. He is quietly standing holding a large ring that has access cards and keys attached to it.

Gabby is feeling a little drunk. She shakes her head in disbelief of what she is seeing. She thinks she is a little confused or she thinks maybe it's just the feeling of utter tiredness from the long night that had just come to an end.

She turns her face away from the worker. She puts Johnathan behind her. She walks into the elevator, "Tomorrow then... another day another dollar...." She thinks tomorrow everything will be better again.

Chapter 18: The Writer

A few weeks go by, and Gabby is caught up in the monotony of life at the hotel.

She is sitting at the hotel lounging area reading a book.

A young man about her age sits on one of the chairs. He is wearing a military shirt and jacket.

There are a few minutes of silence, and the young gentleman breaks the silence. He says, "Hi! I'm Peter! How are you doing this evening?"

Gabby is pleased that Peter wanted to talk. "I'm Gabby, I'm doing fine. How are you?"

He says, "Good. Reading anything good?"

Gabby says, "Yes, a great mystery novel. Right about now, I'm wondering when the killer is going to get caught."

Peter silently smiles. He remains quiet. Gabby closes her book, and she says, "Are you staying at the hotel long?"

Peter says, "Not long, just two nights, I'm waiting for my flight. Going off to boot camp."

Gabby says, "Oh? Will you be away for long?"

Peter says, "Eight years."

Gabby says, "How sad. No girl I guess?"

Peter replies, "No. I don't have a girl, no. But that doesn't mean I can't have one."

Gabby says, "You're leaving though. How would you be able to keep a relationship?"

Peter replies, "I could write."

The two spend a few minutes trading thoughts until Peter asks her to come up to his room with him.

Gabby accepts the invitation.

They spend the night together.

Chapter 19: The Letter

A few weeks pass and a letter arrives for Gabby in the lobby. She received a call in her room, and the letter is delivered to her at her room's door.

The letter is from Peter, the soldier.

Dear Gabby,

> *Greetings from South Carolina. My apologies for not writing to you earlier, but I wasn't allowed to communicate with anyone yet.*

> *You are all I've been thinking about this whole time I've been away.*

> *My Drill Sargent has been teaching me how to be a strong and resistant soldier. That's what I've been: strong and resisting the distance between us.*

> *It's like I said, we can continue our relationship together. All we have to do is write letters so the distance isn't so great.*

> *I've been really lonely here without you. I can't wait for when I am able to see you again. Write back to me, please. Let me know how you are doing there at the hotel.*

Miss you,
Peter Woodhill

Chapter 20: Long Distance

Gabby reads the letter and is extremely flattered. Her reaction though is a bit harsh.

She decides to crunch up the letter into a ball and throw it in the trash. She's still upset about her ex-boyfriend Johnathan. Peter showed up right after the Johnathan break-up, and it was really quick with Peter. She was still getting over Johnathan. Her feelings for him still lingered.

She felt that she also wasn't ready for a long-distance relationship.

Chapter 21: Lover's Quarrel

A male guest had just checked into the hotel. He was there to vent. He needed to give himself some time to reflect on his thoughts. He had just got into a fight with wife. He had just separated from her, left his house, and checked into the hotel.

On the evening he checked into the hotel he sees Gabby walking out of her room.

His room is down the hall from Gabby's room.

She was headed to the bar on the second floor.

The man remembers walking past the second floor bar when he checked in. He decides to go there for a drink. He felt that he would really enjoy one.

Both the male guest and Gabby get on the elevator at the same time.

While inside the elevator the man asks Gabby, "Which floor?"

Gabby says, "Second." The man pushes the button to reach the second floor.

He asks her, "Are you going to the bar?"

Gabby replies, "Yes. Going to grab myself something sweet to drink."

They walk out of the elevator and walk close to each other until they both reach the bar.

They sit close to each other. He offers to buy her a drink.

She asks for a Shirley Temple.

Gabby asks, "Are you planning on staying long?"

He answers, "Just tonight hopefully. I just got into a huge fight with my wife." The man is already mostly resolved. He continues, "I'm going to make it up to her though. I'm going to take her on a vacation and tell her that I'm going to help her with the housework."

That night, Gabby goes back to her room alone. She lays on her bed, and she recalls once upon a time when she was young and she had fallen in love. Although the relationship ultimately didn't work out, she lived a long romance. Her lover back then had made her his only attraction, and she only wanted to be with him. She didn't have any experience with being with someone that had stuck together with her through thick and thin, who loved her that much, like as the man on the hotel's bar that had been sitting next to her. He had someone that he wanted and was special to him. He seemed to love his wife. He wanted to go back to her.

Where had her romances gone?

When was she going to find love again?

Chapter 22: The Hook-Up

It's a Thursday evening, and Gabby meets a blonde guy while she is sitting at the bar. He introduces himself as Casey.

He sits at the bar having a beer while engaging in conversation with Gabby. He is filling Gabby's ears talking about his ex-girlfriend whom he was about to marry for a long period of time. It seemed like it had been two hours that he was describing their relationship and how it ended.

He sounded like he was getting over her still. He got deep about his emotions and how heartbroken he was. He asked Gabby to come up to his room with him.

Gabby was feeling sympathetic to the man's heartbreak and said yes to his offer.

They spent that night together.

Once their union was over, she went back to her room.

In the morning she went to eat breakfast. When she was eating at the restaurant on the first floor, Gabby spotted Casey walking by.

She wondered how long he was going to be staying at the hotel and asked him, "Did you check out yet?"

Casey stopped for a minute and sat down. He has a lot to explain to Gabby, "I called my fiancée this morning, and we're getting back together."

Gabby's stomach churns. She is extremely surprised. She acts as though she isn't hurt and manages to say something in reply. She continues, "How did you manage that?"

He says, "I told her that I didn't mean to hurt her. And that I thought our relationship was worth saving."

Chapter 23: The Wedding Party

A few days later, Casey and his bride to be booked their wedding festivities at the hotel where Gabby and Casey had their affair.

Gabby walks by the banquet hall as their party is taking place, and she sees Casey doing his couple's dance with his brand-new bride in the hotel's spacious room.

Chapter 24: Darkness

Gabby goes through a period of darkness. She feels a distaste for her current luck. She lays in her hotel room with the curtains closed.

It's the weekend, and the day has just begun.

She moves from her bed to sit in her room's sofa chair. She cries while she is sitting on her room chair. Her mood was extremely affected by Casey's decision. He hadn't meant a whole lot to her. They had only just met. She thought that after she had made a connection with him, he would have considered taking things further. Instead, he decided to pick things back up with his fiancée. That was not the result Gabby was expecting.

She feels utter loneliness.

Chapter 25: Baseball Season

The night dawns, and she is calmer. She decides to go down to the lounge where there are chairs to sit on. She plans to sip on a drink while she is there. Gabby goes down to the main bar and grabs a Shirley Temple. She is in the mood to sip on something a little sweet.

A man is sitting at the lounge chair by himself, drinking a beer, and gazing at his phone.

The lounge is a sitting area located a little away from the bar.

Gabby walks to the lounging area. She heads towards a seat.

The man looks up at her and Gabby says, "Hi!" while Gabby is quietly sitting down. She gives him a smile.

The man's mood rises to engage with her.

Gabby's beauty startles him.

He raises his hand to introduce himself, "I'm Henry."

Gabby asks, "Hi Henry! Pleased to meet you. Are you here for long?"

Henry replies, "I'm a baseball player. I'm here for the season. What's your name?"

Gabby introduces herself.

They finish with the introductions. He continues to hold his gaze while looking at her for a few more moments and doesn't say anything else. Gabby starts to feel a little intimidated by the silent stare.

She decides to break the silence, "What?" she voices out.

Henry replies, "Gosh! You are so pretty!"

She giggles and she says, "Thanks."

Henry says, "Could I buy you a drink?"

Gabby says, "Ok."

They get up and walk towards the bar where they order some drinks.

Once the night is over, they both walk back to Gabby's room, and they spend the night together.

Their relationship continues for the extent of the baseball season. He had a few games to play, and he was from out of state.

A few days before Henry was set to leave town, he tells Gabby to come to his room that he has something to talk to her about.

Henry tells her he was out the previous night in his car with another girl.

He tells Gabby that he made out with another girl for a long time and that then he had sex with her.

Henry explains with all openness to Gabby that while he was "doing it" with the other girl, he shouted out the name "Gabby" right in front of the other girl.

Henry said, "I realized then that I had made a mistake."

Henry asked Gabby, "Would you take me back?"

Gabby had been with him for several weeks now.

"Of course not!" she answered him.

Henry pleads, "Come on baby? We're a homerun!"

Gabby answers, "No Henry, I think you hit a ball to the left field and now you are out!" She left his room and slammed the door behind her.

She refused to answer his calls after that.

Chapter 26: Mystery Worker

Gabby is alone for a while. She refuses to get into any more boy trouble. The hotel workers are becoming familiar with her.

She had been staying at the hotel for almost a year.

She can pretty much tell what everyone's role in the building is.

Except for one hotelier. He seems to do all the jobs. The godly handsome looking one. Sometimes he's out front talking to the guests. Sometimes he's picking up luggage and putting it in the wheeled luggage cart.

Sometimes he's looking at her.

Gabby doesn't think she's in trouble, but he looks at her.

She's seen him at the front desk. She's seen him walking through the floors.

Gabby begins to conclude that he must be the hotel manager.

Gabby is coming back from work on a Sunday night. Outside the hotel is the attractive male hotelier.

He was standing before the entry flight of stairs. He says to Gabby, "Hello! Welcome back Ms. Martinez! Can I get you anything to make your evening more pleasant?"

Gabby says, "No, I'm fine thank you! You know my name! I don't know yours."

He wore so many uniforms, Gabby didn't think he ever remembered to put a name tag on.

He says, "My name is Adrian Smith."

Gabby says, "I've noticed you around. Are you the manager?"

Adrian answers, "I'm not the manager exactly, but I'm like the manager. I hold a different position here. I don't exactly have a title."

Gabby feels a little audacious and decides to ask him, "Do you have a break coming up soon?"

Adrian tells her, "Yes. I could take one right now. May I buy you a drink?"

They walk side by side up the short flight of stairs. He signals to her to sit on a couch chair off to the side of the long bar. "I'll go grab you a drink, why don't you wait for me there?"

Gabby walks over to the lounge section of stuffed couch chairs. Before Adrian walks away, he continues to say, "What would you like to drink?"

Gabby answers, "A Washington Apple."

Adrian walks over to the bar. He orders two drinks. He brings the drinks over to where Gabby is waiting.

They both stare at one another for a few moments. Gabby is very attracted to the gentleman who had remained mysterious the entire time she had been staying at the hotel.

He asks her, "Where do you go off to work all day?"

Gabby answers, "I'm a manager at a department store that sells clothes. It's a little ways away from this city. The company has other stores all over the Bay Area."

Adrian is amused. He's noticed Gabby over the past several months. Sometimes she's alone. Sometimes she's not. He's noticed her go through several relationships while she's been checked into this hotel. She never seems to check out.

They sit and talk for longer. They indulge in each other's company.

Adrian doesn't open up about himself right away. Instead, he just listens to Gabby talk.

It doesn't take too many Washington Apples to make Gabby a little tipsy.

Chapter 28: The Hotelier

Before the night is over, Gabby seduces the hotelier into her room. He follows to the third floor and goes inside her room. She takes off her warm California Wear clothing line sweater she had been wearing.

He gets undressed.

They sleep together.

Once it was all over, the night became peaceful. The hotel was silent. The streets outside were calm.

In the morning he was gone.

Gabby thought about him, "Back to work I guess, I hope he had a good time."

Chapter 29: The Game

It's another evening at Gabby's multi-floor home. She is off from work while on a different floor of the lavish hotel building. The man dressed in a concierge outfit pulls his key ring out and selects a card key. He invites her into his room.

The 21st floor corner suite is the largest she's ever seen. The carpet is different in this room. It's black and cream with wavy squarish vine designs. The chairs were gold and erect with deep cushions. A love seat stooped in the room. The dresser had a smooth finish that was a deep black with a flashy white lining.

A beautiful glass table stood off to the right. Adrian walks in to place his key ring on top of the glass table.

As he walks in with her he introduces himself a little better. "My father owns this hotel."

She can see the bedroom in the other room. A balcony stands beyond it.

Adrian decides to say more about himself, "I look over all that happens here. Sometimes I let guests check into this suite. It's the presidential suite. It stays empty most of the time. I like to use it for my personal needs."

They sat down in the front room.

They talked about work, they talked about their finances, and they talked about what they both wanted out of life.

She said, "I want to be in a committed relationship."

Adrian says, "I'm game. As long as you're staying here at the hotel."

Chapter 30: The Date

Their first night going steady they went to a comedy club. The show was advertised in the local paper.

The line outside the venue stretched far. It went up a long flight of stairs. Several young and middle-aged adults stood in line.

Adrian paid for their entry. They ordered the required minimum drink purchase.

The show had talent. Gabby hadn't laughed for such a long time.

The night was memorable. They returned to the hotel. Adrian took her up to his preferred suite.

Chapter 31: Extended Stay

After Adrian noticed that Gabby had been staying at his hotel for several consecutive months, he began to grow an interest in her. He also noticed that Gabby never seemed to leave the hotel at night.

He wanted to do something different with her. He wanted to gain her interest. The night at the comedy club was a well-planned out date he had made with her. It had gone really well.

He wanted to take her out of the hotel more than just once.

There were lots of places he could take her to out on the city.

Chapter 32: The City

Adrian asked Gabby if she could take a weekend off so they could explore the city.

He took her to the pier. They walked the busy sidewalk drinking a milkshake.

They acted like tourists and bought foggy city shirts.

They kissed.

<h1 style="text-align:center">Chapter 33: Selfie</h1>

They walked along the sidewalk that borders the cold ocean water. Gabby poses for a picture. She smiles at the good-looking man that has taken an interest in her.

She considers her beauty. She always attracts a companion. They never want to continue to stay with her, though, for a long while.

They take a selfie.

They snap more photos.

When Gabby got a chance, she took her phone to a pharmacy to get her pictures developed. She purchased an album and started making a photo book she was certain she was going to keep.

Chapter 35: Dinner

Adrian took her out for another enchanted evening. They ate dinner in a restaurant that was only a few paces off from the hotel.

They stopped in at a bar playing loud music. They sat down and talked for a while.

Chapter 36: Another Day Off

It was Gabby's day off again. She looked for Adrian while she arrived at the hotel. She glanced towards the front desk and noticed that he wasn't there.

She approached Meredith, who worked in the front desk, and said, "Hey Meredith! Would you happen to know where I could find Adrian?"

Meredith answered, "He's up on the tenth-floor in room 111 talking to Joanne the cleaning lady."

Gabby took the elevator up to the tenth floor in search for Adrian.

Once she found him, she made a slow approach so as not to disturb Adrian while he was conducting his duties.

Adrian finished giving instructions on last minute tasks he expected the cleaning lady to complete before the night is over.

He turns to Gabby and greets her, "Hello! How are you this evening?"

"Tired. I need a shower and a few minutes of meditating." She looks inside the room that Joanne is cleaning, "Wow! What an awesome room! Look at that bed!" She stares at the large king size bed inside the room.

Gabby teases, "Have you ever slept in that bed before?"

Adrian replies in a serious voice, "No. Not that one." He's quiet for a moment, and he decides to continue the conversation. They are both still in the presence of Joanne, but she's in the distance.

While standing outside the room with the door open, Adrian whispers to Gabby, "Would you like to sleep in each different style room we have at the hotel? We can try all the bed sizes."

Gabby answers, "Yes. When do we start?"

Chapter 37: Bed Sizes

They started that night after the cleaning lady was done. Adrian informed Joanne that he would be staying there that night and that it would need service in the morning. Joanne the cleaning lady acknowledged this.

Chapter 38: Envelopes

The playfulness began.
Each night he dropped an envelope with a room number and key under her room door.

Chapter 39: Chocolate Strawberries

On the second night, they entered a room that was different in style. Adrian spiced it up and had a box of chocolate covered strawberries placed on each of the beds of the double bed room.

They made out and went to bed with each other on each bed. They did it twice, once in each bed.

Chapter 40: The Wall

On the third night, Adrian selected a room that had no view. It was facing a brick wall. That room had a bottle of champagne on ice chilling on the night stand. This was one of the rooms with a less extravagant view.

Adrian met Gabby in a different room every night for several weeks.

In the mornings, they went back to their respective rooms.

They went back to their respective lives.

Adrian always stayed at the hotel. Gabby went to sell California Wear clothes at her regular job, the clothing line that she always undressed from when she got back to where she would sleep for the night.

Chapter 42: The Other Home

Adrian occasionally left the hotel. He owned a home a little way away from the downtown of the big city.

He had a Porsche he kept parked in the parking garage outside the hotel. He paid monthly dues to keep his car there.

He often stayed at the hotel months at a time and just went back home to take some time off.

Chapter 43: His House

Adrian's house was in another district of the city. It was a quieter area where two story houses stood. It was hard to notice the house's prettiness because there were a lot of trees and bushes surrounding it.

Chapter 44: The Bachelor

When Adrian the bachelor had met Gabby, he hadn't dated anyone in several years. He was only interested in making the hotel perform at its best.

The last relationship he had been in was back in high school. Things didn't go the way he had wanted them to go, and he hadn't meet another girl since.

He was in his mid-twenties now, and Gabby was quite alluring. Her looks, her smile, and her candor all enticed him.

Chapter 45: Breakfast

Morning breakfast was much cozier since Adrian had come around.

Gabby showers and gets ready. She takes the elevator down and walks into the restaurant on the first floor of the hotel.

She sits on a table and waits for Adrian. He usually eats the meal together with her.

He occasionally is held back dealing with a situation in the hotel.

Chapter 46: Changes

Gabby came back from work one evening and walked into her room.

She showered and got her clothes from the hotel laundry bag.

She knew that Adrian was busy right then.

She sat by herself contemplating her life.

Adrian had been dating her for some time. A long time. They were currently in a romance of sorts. He was taking her out to dates, and she was totally into him.

She was generally feeling better about life and how things were turning out.

Chapter 47: The Hall

One evening Adrian decides to impress Gabby and sets up the event hall with one table and all the fancy dinnerware the hotel has to offer. He orders catering and invites Gabby for a candlelit dinner.

He dresses in a suit rather than his hotel wear. He brings out the chivalry and seats her in her chair.

They share a romantic dinner. They discuss their day. He asks her where she sees their relationship going.

Gabby answers, "Wherever you want it to go. You know me. I'm not going to lie. I've been around. I can't even hide it from you. You saw me going through man after man here in the hotel. It just didn't work out with any of them. I'm extremely happy with you. The more I get to know you the more I like you. I'd like to see through where this will lead."

Adrian asks Gabby, "Will you marry me?"

Gabby says, "Yes."

Chapter 48: Wedding Plans

Gabby is busy for the next few weeks making wedding plans. She begins to write down a list of guests that would be coming to the super private wedding she wanted to have. She asked Adrian for a list of all his employees, who were surely going to be invited. She was stuck for a moment when she began to consider her family.

She decided to call her mom and attempt a reconciliation.

Once the phone call was over— two hours later— her mother was added to the invitation list.

Chapter 49: The Dress

She went out of town to a wedding dress shop she had heard about.

The mall where the dress shop was located was mostly empty. There were a few stragglers, but it looked deserted.

This mall was in an expensive area. All the shops had products that cost a lot of money. She was aware of that.

She walked into the dress shop and waited to be helped.

Once she found someone to help her, the customer service lady handed her a magazine. The service lady told her to pick a dress and tell her what she wanted.

Gabby took several minutes to make a selection and presented it to the woman who worked in the shop. The woman told Gabby to leave her phone number so she could let her know what the price of the dress would be.

Gabby went back to the hotel and waited for the return phone call.

She waited for two weeks. No return phone call ever came.

Gabby decided to go with something a little simpler. She walked into a well-known retail franchise of wedding dresses.

She picked out a dress and bought it on the spot.

Chapter 50: Silent Owner

Adrian organized a family luncheon. He invited his mother and his father.

Adrian had been keeping his father informed of his relationship with Gabby from the moment it had started.

It was at the family luncheon that Gabby was first introduced to the hotel's silent owner.

Adrian was the one who did all the work. His father, the hotel's actual owner did little himself. He had long retired from the position he had handed over to his son. He had taught his son all that he knew about the hotel business. He had left it up to his son, Adrian, to run the hotel. It was Adrian's job to make sure things continued to run smoothly.

Chapter 51: Wedding Ceremony

The church was filled with 200 guests. Their ceremony was recorded on a video camera.

There were cars that took the guests from the church to the hotel's party hall.

Gabby got to have her first dance with her groom Adrian in the infamous banquet hall she had recalled having crossed while it was full of people on one occasion several months earlier.

Chapter 52: Open Bar

The second floor's bar was offering free drinks to all the wedding guests, many of whom stayed in the hotel rooms of the upper floors following the lovely event.

The night of the wedding, Adrian took Gabby to his home in the suburbs of the city. They spent their wedding night there.

Chapter 54: Perks

From then on, she got to choose whether she would stay in the spacious home or the hotel's presidential suite. It was up to her.

Chapter 55: Choices

Gabby was in limbo about returning to her job. She had taken an extended vacation and had just come back from her honeymoon. She wasn't sure she wanted to continue working.

She wanted to have a baby.

Chapter 56: The News

The month after Gabby and Adrian were married, Gabby sees that the baseball player is back in town. He has checked into the hotel. He is not aware of the changes that have taken place since he has left. The baseball player sees that Gabby is walking around the second floor's lobby by herself.

Henry, the baseball player, turns from his drink at the bar and asks Gabby, "Hey, are you down to bat?"

Gabby has a flash back to her old life. She understands how Henry couldn't possibly know that she is not the same girl he met so long ago.

Gabby thinks about how Henry has not found love yet. She tells him, "No thanks Henry. I'm a married woman now. Just walking by."

Henry utters, "Married! Psh! Congrats!" He turns back towards the bar. He thinks to himself, in the end, all we all want is to find someone to love, someone to cherish. Maybe I'll find the woman I'm looking for. Like Gabby had found the one for her. Maybe I'll end up getting married too. I just have to keep trying. Love isn't impossible to find. It may just take a few tries.

www.ingramcontent.com/pod-product-compliance
Lightning Source LLC
Chambersburg PA
CBHW050804160726
48004CB00002B/699